copyright

Disclaimer

This is a work of fiction. Names, characters, organizations, spots, occasions and occurrences are either the results of the creator's creative energy or utilized as a part of an invented way. Any similarity to real people, living or dead, or genuine occasions is absolutely adventitious.

ISBN:
ebook: 978-1-946792-18-1
print:978-1-946792-19-8
audio/d :978-1-946792-20-4

© 2017 Urquhart Randolph

Published by Glofton llc

Table of Contents

VISIT US

WWW.GLOFTON.COM
Enroll in our VIP list.
Be the first to be notified on our latest published book.
Downloading for free gifts.

EGO PROBLEM WITH SEXY SCARS

Chapter 1

"Please sit and follow the instructions given to you. The airplane will take off in a few minutes." This and hundreds of other instructions were given to passengers before a flight. I didn't listen to anyone; I was just sitting there and thinking about my plan. I wanted to make a perfume for women that will be so strong, that men will simply be unable to resist women using it.

I knew that I had to go to South America to search for plants that will eventually serve as extracts for my perfume.

I was so excited about it until something interrupted my thoughts and excitement. "Sir, here is your meal, take it, please. "Stewardess said as she inclined toward me to put the food on my table. I was so turned on by her boobs, that If I changed my look to her eyes that were heaven-colored, I would go even higher in the sky and eventually I would fall in love.

Well, maybe I wouldn't fall in love, maybe I would fall on her boobs again. However, I didn't look at food nor did I listen to any of her words because her boobs distracted me.

"I hope you enjoy the flight. If you need something, don't hesitate to call me." Even though I wasn't hungry, I removed the cover of the plate and I started eating. Something made me spit the food. The food was delicious and it didn't make me spit my bite, but the content of the paper did.

"Come to the cockpit, I want to feel your cock - Lucy, the stewardess that made her boobs visible only for you." That was the stewardess that brought me the food." I wiped my mouth with a tissue, made my suit neat and I set my feet on the passage between rows. I was walking toward the cockpit with a smile on my face.

When I came in, there were two women flying the plane, and Lucy. Lucy was the stewardess that I immediately recognized. She was standing against the inner surface of the plane and rubbed her pussy. She had only her shirt on. She put her forefinger in her mouth.

"Why didn't you come earlier? I was wondering if you were going to come." Said Lucy.

"You can't imagine what I'm going to do to your body. When Eugene fucks, Eugene goes deep." I said.

Anyway, I gave myself some preparation here. Now I'm all yours. Do whatever you want with my body." She said this as she was spreading her hands as she wanted to say "I don't want to do anything here, you're the leader".

I started stripping my clothes off. I couldn't untie my tie. She disappeared for few minutes and she came back with scissors. The first thing that she did was put the scissors inside her pussy.

"I want you to have a trace of my body on your clothes." She wiped the scissors off my shirt and the next moment the liquid from inside of her pussy was visible on my shirt. After that, she cut my tie and once again she moved to the inner surface of the plane.

"I'm all yours once again, come and get what you came for."

This girl was turning me on for real. I stripped off my shirt and that moment sky lost its beauty because the biggest beauty right there were my muscles. It's not that I like to brag about them, but every girl that saw them said that she had never seen so big muscles with such sharp and sexy definitions.

My chest was so big that drops of water used to be jealous after I would take the shower. Moving down, my abs were so well developed that drops would stuck between two packs of abdominal muscles. Two lines, each of them placed at the two opposite sides under my abs were long, and suck deep inside my skin.

"Oh my God, I didn't know that you're so hot. The challenge of you doing whatever you want to me is over. She moved away from the wall, embraced my neck with her right shoulder as her left hand touched my abs. She was kissing me with such a passion.

I had a feeling that I was in paradise even though I was on fire, which is typical for hell. My body was hell, no girl ever resisted to my body. "Oh my god, look at the size." She said as one of the girls piloting plane took a look at my dick.

"Oh my god. Look at the shape. It has a better shape than this plane has." Said the other girl. She ripped off her shirt, put my head on her breast and I started licking like someone forced me to do it like that. I just couldn't resist but to lick every little part of her breast. She raised her head as she sighed. I put my forefinger inside her genitals and started fingering her really hard.

She was screaming like crazy. I glanced at her which were half-closed. She seemed like she's in the seventh sky. We were in the sky, but far away from the seventh sky.

Her eyes were almost closed, like she was about to pass out, but she was still conscious, screaming and holding her hands at my muscular shoulder. She was kissing a tattooed place on my shoulder, I guess that astonished caused by the amazing shape of my muscles keep her conscious. I put my finger out of her vagina, took her whole body in my hands and kissed her slowly as she was lying in my hands horizontally.

I was kissing her with passion as she looked at my eyes with a big smile, just as she was in love. Her eyes were telling me that she didn't regret risking her job because of sex.

I laid her on the floor as I spread her hands widely. I was kissing her all the way from her lips to her genitals. Finally, when I reached genitals I spread the opening of it a little bit.

"You're letting my penis come in on your own wish. The space that you have here is enough for an average dick, but not for a dick of my size."

She just kept on smiling and nodded "yes" with her head. I put my tongue inside her vagina, and even though it was wet I made it even wetter.

She was screaming so much that one of the passengers knocked on the door of the cockpit and asked if everything is okay in the cockpit.

"There is nothing to worry about, sir. It's just that my colleague is having a migraine." Said one of the pilots."

"All right then. I thought that something is wrong with the plane." Replied the passenger

"Everything is okay sir. Enjoy the flight." Said one of the pilots.

I started putting it inside slowly, I didn't put even a half of it and she already started screaming like crazy. I put my hand on her mouth to stop the scream. Her eyes were widely opened. I asked her if she wants me to put the whole size inside. She nodded "yes" with her head.

I put the whole size of my penis inside. She shed a few tears but she didn't want me to stop. I was going slow and with the whole size. She was screaming when I started speeding up. I was coming inside and out of her body.

We were together, two bodies connected one to another and flying in the metal tube called airplane.

I've reached the maximal speed. I fucked her so hard that her tears were going in the direction of her boobs. She picked up those tears from her boobs and she rubbed her pussy with her hand. I put my penis outside and let her rest a bit. She was shaking as she was in the cold water. There was no place for cold notions such as water because everything was hot and I wanted to make it even hotter by going anal

She was lying on the floor with her boobs against the floor as I was lying on her body, touching her boobs and squeezing them, just like baker squeezes the dough. I moved my hands to her pussy and started massaging it slowly. Her tone was lowered this time since I was the man who knows how to go gently with massage. Two girls that were piloting the plane were looking at me, their face showed that they were amazed by what was I doing to Lucy.

"Hey, focus on the piloting. We will get his cock once she was done." Said one of the girls to her pilot colleague."

"I don't know how to fly." Said Lucy.

"But you are already flying in heaven, aren't you?" I said as I put my dick inside her vagina, this time the whole size of it."

"Oh yeah." She said with a prolonged scream.

Every once in awhile I had to put my dick outside because her orgasm-liquid was coming out of her pussy. I was really on fire. I was showing her what I really can do. I ejaculated on her boobs. She didn't stop screaming not even after I ejaculated. I irritated her pussy so much.

After she recovered a little bit, she put her shirt and her professional jacket on and she sat down to help piloting the plane.

Of Course, she didn't pilot it, but she was just sitting there in the case that someone comes up. From the back, she looked the same as her colleague Josie, whom I started undressing. Josie was a tall and handsome girl.

I had enough strength to satisfy needs of five more women, so it wasn't a problem for me to go as hard as I did previously.

At the same wet place where I screwed Lucky, Josie was lying with me on her body. I had my whole hand inside her body, but she wasn't screaming as much as Lucy did.

After licking each of the parts of her body, she put it in her mouth. The pleasure was big but I wanted to make it even bigger, so I took her beautiful red hair in my hand and pushed my dick all the way to her throat. Soon, her mouth was slobbery.

I put the middle part of her body on a chair, spread her legs and put them on my shoulders as I put my tongue inside her vagina. A sudden big scream resounded the cockpit. Of Course, it was Josie screaming.

I was simply a man who loved action. Putting it inside made her screaming but she wasn't screaming as much as Lucy did. Her legs were by my hips and my dick was inside her.

It lasted for an hour. I was lying on the floor as I needed just a few minutes to regain some strength. Alisha was the last one who got it. After the intercourse, Alisha simply couldn't get off my muscles. She was licking it all the way, before the intercourse and after it. After that sex, I didn't want to go back to the place where rest of the passengers were.

Instead, I approached to each of the three girls and licked their pussies. They had their shirts and jackets on, but they were naked down there. I enjoyed each of them. It was a beautiful experience, not only for them but for me too.

Lucy wanted to do it once again, so we started the action. In the middle of sex, something went wrong. The airplane started crashing. The airplane was falling down and everyone was screaming, running around and searching for help.

Lucy and I didn't move, I was going as hard as I could on her not caring about how painful it was for her because we were all about to die. A few moments after both of us ejaculated, the plane crashed. The next moment I was unconscious.

"Will somebody pull my leg out, please. Someone come and pull my leg out!" I heard this voice, but everything was obscure in front of me. Soon, I started seeing things. Smoke was all over the plane, but it was visible enough for me to see all that mess. Blood was all over the place. I approached the man that asked for help, and I pulled his leg out. It was stuck under the fire extinguisher that was under one of the seats. Except us, nobody survived. We were still far away from South America. We were on some kind of the island.

We got out of the plane and the first thing that we searched for was water. There was some water inside the plane, but we couldn't come back since the plane was on fire. After thirty minutes of walking and seeing a lot of animals, we saw a snake. It was a very big snake, I wouldn't be able to name the exact kind.

However, the snake was stretched over our passage through woods. We couldn't take any other way since the grass was too big. If we decided to go another way, we would have probably met another snake, and we would get bitten.

"Well, not the best situation to ask about your name, but you haven't told me yet." I said to the man.

"My name is Roy." Said he.

"My name is Eugene, nice to meet you, Roy," I said while my face looked very scared, and indeed, I was scared.

"How do we get ourselves out of this situation Roy?"

"Well, look at that snake, it would love to bite us more than anyone."

"Maybe it's because we are the only ones on this island, and it didn't bite anybody for a long time."

"Well, let's search for some rocks." Said Roy.

"That's a good idea."

So we went back to search for some rocks, but for some reason, we couldn't find any rocks. We tried to figure out something else. We found a tree that was half-cut by the thunder.

I took the black fried side of the tree, whereas my friend took the opposite side. We were carrying that tree and walking toward the snake. We had a plan to throw that tree on the snake and to kill it that way. When we came back, we didn't see any snake.

"What is this?" Asked Roy.

"I guess that we didn't come back to the right place. Maybe we should go a little bit further."

We continued walking but we couldn't see any snake. We dropped off the tree that we were holding.

"Huh. I can't believe that we were carrying this tree almost a mile and there is no snake." Said Rob.

"Be happy that snake has gone. What if another snake joined that snake, and this tree wasn't enough for both of them." I said to Rob.

"When you look at the things that way, you're right."

We continued walking the island, but we couldn't find any water.

"Oh, shit. What is this man, the water is so bitter." Said the man as he drank a little bit of ocean water. We must find some pure water before it gets too dark to see anything.

We walked the whole day and we finally found a place where water was dripping, but in small quantities. Anyway, it was enough for us to have our daily needs met.

We were discovering the ocean with the emotions of fear and curiosity mixed up. We didn't know where on earth we were. At the end of the day, we were sitting on a hill that was just by the ocean.

"What do you think, do boats sail nearby this island?" Asked Roy.

"We will never know until we see. We will have to sit here and stare at the ocean until something shows up."

"What if nothing shows up?" Asked Roy.

"Well, that's a tough question."

We spent two hours just staring at the ocean and waiting for something to show up, but nothing did.

When we woke up, we were thinking about what to eat. Roy came up with an idea.

"We should make a catch and get some bird inside of it."

I didn't have a better idea, so we came to search for something that was of a cubical shape. Maybe someone was here, maybe someone left something on the island. We were discovering the island, but we couldn't find anything. We were frightened more than ever. If nobody has ever been there, then nobody managed to leave this place. How are we supposed to leave it then? A lot of thoughts were crossing my worried mind.

"Man, stop worrying, we will find a way out of this misery". I can't think straight If I'm hungry. We found some big and thick plants. We were wrapping the plants one in another, and after two hours of struggle, we managed to make something that looked like a cylinder.

We pulled fibers out of Roy's clothes and tied that cylinder. We managed to dig up some worms, and we put the worms under our "plant-cylinder".

Holding the cylinder with the fibers, we hid inside undergrowth. We were waiting two hours for some bird to come, but we didn't see any bird. We quit that idea. Once again we were sitting on the same hill.

"Man, I'm so hungry." Said Roy.

"So am I, but we will figure something out."

"Let's try fishing. We must catch something, either bird or fish. Otherwise, we will die my friend." I said.

We decided to use the same cylinder that we used for catching birds.

Fortunately, we caught some fishes and at the end of the day, we were full.

Next morning when we woke up we decided to go for a walk. We decided to discover every little place on the island.

During our walk, we were chatting.

"Roy, your beard is so big."

"I don't worry about the beard. What I'm actually worried about is that I'm going to grow old here."

"No, don't worry about that. It's not that bad. You're not going to grow old here."

"You think so?"

"Yeah. Actually, you're going to die here.

"Thanks for compassion friend."

"I'm joking, don't take it seriously. I said to Roy.

Chapter 2

Walking the island, we noticed a cave. We wanted to explore it a little bit, so we walked in. I couldn't believe what I saw. There was Lucy inside. As soon as I saw her, I gave her a hug.

"I can't believe that you're there, I thought that I was all alone on this island." Said Lucy.

"Well, we thought that only two of us are on this island." We were walking together the whole day.

"Do you sleep inside the cave?" Roy asked Lucy.

"Yes, I do."

"And is it too cold inside?" I asked Lucy.

"No, nights are very hot outside, and inside the cave it is just perfect."

"May we join you? Because we're sleeping under a tree." I asked Lucy.

"It would be my pleasure. I would love it!"

"Thank you very much." Said Roy.

Rest of the day, we spent walking and talking.

"Tell me, how come you survived? You were unconscious and you were bleeding. The plane even exploded just a few minutes after we left it."

"I know that it exploded, it exploded only two minutes after I left it. Anyway, I'm happy that I'm with you guys."

"We're happy that we found you." I said as I looked at Roy.

"If we want to eat tonight, we must go fishing." Said Rock.

"Well, that makes sense. Let's go fishing." Said Lucy.

We were fishing and we were very successful.

Lighting the fire was a real struggle. We were scratching a rock over another rock, and it really was a long process.

Nevertheless, we managed to light the fire. We baked the fish and twenty minutes later, we were full. We went to the cave, and even though during other nights it wasn't hot inside, during this night it was. That was the reason that we couldn't sleep. We were talking jokes and laughing a lot.

We would reveal each other our deepest secrets. That is how it looks like when you don't know if you're ever going to come back to your place.

In those two hours that we spent talking, I found out about Roy and Lucy more than I knew about some of my friends that I met a few years ago. However, talking wasn't enough.

Our bodies were full of fat and we had to do some physical activity to burn the fat. I slowly approached Lucy. I sat down on the floor, with my back against the wall. I laid her in my arms as I started unbuttoning her shirt.

"Oh. What are you doing?" Said she while smiling.

"I don't know, what do you think I'm doing?"

"You know that we're not alone now?" She said.

"I didn't know that you guys are so close." Said Roy.

Roy was also a muscular guy.

"It doesn't matter, Roy can join us too, if you want?"

"Two dicks is always better than one. Isn't it right?"

"I know that two pussies are better than one. We don't care about dicks, except for our own dicks."

When I said this, we all laughed as I unbuttoned her shirt completely. She had nothing under the shirt. I was holding her round breast once again in my hands. While she was lying in my arms, she raised her head and started kissing me. I was touching her boobs as she kissed me.

Roy joined us and stripped Lucy's pants and everything she was wearing. He had his tongue in her vagina as I had my dick in her mouth. My hands were on her boobs.

After some time, I replaced my tongue with my penis. It was hard for her to take him inside completely, but going slowly, I made it possible. After that, Roy and I changed our places.

I was having my tongue in her vagina, whereas Roy had his dick inside her mouth. After that, both Roy and I stood up, stripped off and showed our dicks.

We compared it. They were of a similar size. Since conflict between two of us emerged, we asked if Lucy can decide which one is bigger. She put Roy's penis in her mouth, and after that she put mine.

"Both of your dicks are coming to the middle of my throat, they are the same size." Said Lucy.

Roy took his big dick and put it on her breast. He started coming back and forth with it. While he was doing that, I couldn't resist but to go anal on her. She was screaming and I was going harder on her.

The cave resounded the screams. After that, Roy put his dick inside her vagina. The most beautiful part of our muscular and sexy bodies was entering two holes of her body. We had to do it slowly at the beginning because she never had experience like that. She was screaming more than ever.

At the moment both of us had it inside her vagina, and we were pushing slowly. Afterward, I would put it off and he would start going as hard as he could on her vagina.

Then I would go anal as hard as possible. After some practice, we were going as hard as possible simultaneously. She was screaming so hard but her body wasn't shaking because our dicks kept the balance of her body. She was sweating really much. We put it out and we let her rest.

She was holding Roy's penis in one hand as she was jerking it off, and at the same time, she was sucking mine. After that, I spread her legs while she was standing with her boobs against the wall. I was screwing her on my own, and I was going really fast.

During that time, Roy was licking her vagina. After that, we had our dicks in her pussy simultaneously. We were fucking her so hard and so fast that our dicks couldn't be seen.

"Put it out!" She said.

She had an orgasm. There was the liquid going all around. Her orgasm lasted thirty seconds. She collapsed after she was done with her orgasm. Roy and I took a little bit of the liquid that she produced in mouth, and we spit it on her boobs.

Roy and I ejaculated as well, right in her mouth. After few minutes, she was conscious again. She was tired but she never felt better. She had two experienced and muscled guys. She was really lucky to have us.

Sun raised up, and a new day started. Nevertheless, there was something interesting that my eyes caught yesterday. I have seen some interesting plants. They had a shape of roses, and they were black and blue. When I woke up, I decided to go and check it out on my own. I didn't reveal my plan about searching for extracts for my new perfume to anyone. When I came to the field filled with plants, I took one and put it under my nose.

It smelled incredibly good, it turned me on so much that I wanted to go back and screw Lucy again, but If I did that, she wouldn't be able to walk the whole day. Anyway, I was glad that I found something interesting. I had to pick up as many different kinds of plants as possible and take it to my home laboratory.

There was just one problem, how do I get back to my home? Days were passing and we were even more hopeless than the first day on the island. Both Roy and I had a bigger beard, and Lucy was hairy down there. When we would have an intercourse, it would be beard-crash, but it felt really good.

During one of the typical activities where Roy and I would screw Lucy, we saw a boat. It was a huge boat and it was about half of a mile away from the coast. We were standing naked as we waved to the boat. However, nobody paid attention, although there were people standing on the boat's deck. Roy and I raised Lucy on our shoulders and told her to wave, which is what she did.

She was shouting: "Help, help! Someone help us please!" Anyway, she wasn't loud enough so we wanted her to scream more in order to attract attention. That's why I put my tongue inside her pussy as deep as I could. When I did it, she started shouting really loud.

It was a scream that one can hear even if he is a mile away. The boat started changing its direction. It started going toward us. Luckily, I've already cut the plants that I thought would be good for my new perfume.

"You two stay there and I will come back soon." I said.

"What the hell is wrong with you? We finally have a chance to go away from this island and you're going back to the island?" Said Roy.

"I will be back in a few minutes, if the boat arrives before I'm back, tell them to wait for me."

I went to the deepest stage of the cave where I hid my plants, I picked them up and went back to the coast. There was nobody. The only thing that I saw was the boat going away from the coast.

With the sun reflected on my muscles, I was touching my chest with my beard. I was never a desperate man; I always knew that there is a way out. One just has to think hard in order to figure out a solution. I was fishing, sometimes I would even catch a bird. There were some animals that I didn't dare to eat since I wasn't familiar with those species.

At least, I was never lacking sweet food because there was a lot of coconut on the island. Lacking sex was the worst thing. After eating coconut, I would feel like screwing Lucy, but this time she screwed me up by leaving me alone here. It was kinda strange feeling.

You miss the company but at the same time, you realize that people are assholes.

Nobody can hurt you if you're alone on the island. Looking at the sky, animals and sea were the most peaceful things. Looking at the waterfall was for me incredible experience. I was thinking about life more than ever.

Should I come back to my home at all? Maybe I was happy that Roy and Lucy left me here. Animals are politer than people, and raise of the sun is all that existed when the first man settled on earth. The problem with being alone on the island is that you don't have some particular goals. But look, if one chases his goals all the time all the way until he dies, he will never be happy.

I just need to achieve this, and I will be happy. If one accept himself fully in its present shape, he would realize that he isn't missing anything and that he is blessed just for being alive.

Well, that is the way it is. Anyway, my sex drive was too high so I couldn't stay there all alone. I decided to spend some time without thinking of departure, so I could explore the plants.

Chapter 3

While I was among the plants looking for new species, I heard a small helicopter.

"Gary, look! There is somebody down there!" A woman said.

"Well, that is pretty interesting, but you know that we have to work." Said Gary, the pilot."

"Maybe he is stuck there." Said the woman.

"No way, there is something that he came with right there, helicopter, boat, or something else. He will use the same ride to come back."

"Let's fly down to check it. By the way, he is so sexy, look at those muscles." Said the woman as she used a spyglass to spy on me.

I was waving them, and thankfully, they were coming for me.

The more they approached to me, the bigger influence propeller had on my body. The cool air that propeller produced was touching my body so gently that I felt like a woman is touching me.

I was holding a flower in my hand, as the sexy woman exited the helicopter. She was so sexy, In my entire life, I've never seen anything like that. She was 90-60-90. She was wearing a miniskirt so short, that if she lifted it up just a centimeter, her pussy would appear.

Her breast was like two giant coconuts, and the wind was throwing her hair like a man throws pleasure inside a woman body. While propeller had its last movements in the sky, we were looking into each other eyes. We didn't talk because the helicopter was still too loud. She looked at me with such amazement in her eyes, and I looked at her. I was amazed by the way she looked, but I didn't show it on my face.

"Hi, my name is Patricia, and this is Gary."

"Hi, Patricia. Nice to meet you, Gary. My name is Eugene."

"Yeah, nice to meet you pal." Said Gary as he was standing with his back against the helicopter's surface.

"We were wondering what are you doing here all alone." Said Patricia.

"She was wondering if you can screw her, she can't get enough of a dick." Said Gary having his voice lowered.

"Well, I'm not doing anything in particular. I am just walking." I said.

"You came to this island just to walk all alone?" Asked Patricia.

"Well, I don't know if you could see it from above, but there is an airplane wreckage on this island. The airplane crashed, and I was one of the passengers." I said while looking at Patricia.

"Oh, poor man. Look at those scratches." She was looking at my wounded shoulders as she held her hands on it.

"Is there a way for you to come back?" She asked.

"Maybe if someone picks me up. It would be hard to come back on my own."

"That's why we are here. You're coming with us. We will take you back to your home."

"Oh, that's really nice." I picked up my plants and after a few minutes, we reached for the sky.

They were hunters. Before they noticed me, they were heading to some place to hunt animals. Gary was just her partner in hunting. Patricia was sitting next to me in the helicopter, putting on my arm some cream for wounds healing. She was doing it really gently, looking at my eyes. Time by time she would bite her lip.

I couldn't resist, so I started kissing her. She spread her legs and my belly was against her genitals, even though we were not naked yet. I was kissing her as she was jerking my dick off. I pulled the upper part of her t-shirt a little bit down, and I made her shoulder visible. I kissed her mouth, red like a cherry. The next moment, I was kissing her shoulder.

I left traces of lipstick on it. She was so beautiful and so handsome. I stripped her off completely and I put my head on her breast.

"Put your penis between them." She said.

She wasn't the only one that liked to have it between the breast. My dick was so big that starting from above her belly and coming between her breast, my dick would touch her chin. Then she stripped me off.

She was kissing my mouth and going down my neck. Just like every girl, she was astonished by my chest. I didn't know if her lips or hands touched it more. However, I felt really good.

My dick got up so much that it was completely vertical and against my body. It stretched all the way to my navel. After licking my abs, next thing she played with was my penis. She pulled her tongue out and with the peak of it, she licked the little hole in my penis. I was so turned on that my penis turned red.

It was an incredible experience, this girl knew what she was doing. I couldn't believe what was I witnessing at the moment. She put it all the way to her throat. She even put the balls inside. This girl had substantial experience. While she still had it in her mouth, I was thinking how strange it is that I'm having so much of sex in the air. She simply couldn't resist, and she put him inside on her own.

She was sitting on my dick having it inside in its full size. She was jumping on it like it's the last time she was going to get screwed. I stretched my right hand and I put my head on triceps and biceps. Those two muscles were big enough for me to lean my head completely. I was just lying while she did the whole job.

It was a beautiful feeling to be inside her body. She was going so hard on me that even Gary was turned on by looking at her jumping like crazy. She was in that position already for 20 minutes.

I could tell that she was tired, but still, the pleasure of having it inside prevailed over the feeling of tiredness.

"Do you want me to help you?"

"I can do it on my own, but if you want it, go on."

"I lifted her whole body without putting my penis outside her vagina. I was holding her body in a line with my body as I screwed her. A few minutes later, I put him outside for a few seconds, turned her body upside down so she could make my penis wet with her mouth.

We had oral sex. I was having my tongue inside her vagina and it was hard for her to scream since she was assigned the task to suck it. After that, I turned her body in a normal position and I lifted her to my belly once again. I held her legs in my hands to keep the balance of her body. I was going really hard on her.

But what surprised me was the fact that she didn't scream much, she was used to big dicks. Inside the helicopter, above the seats, there was a bar for holding hands on it.

She was hanging there, I spread her legs as much as I could and I put my tongue inside. It was extreme sex. She had an orgasm right there.

The liquid caused by her orgasm was hitting my abdominal muscles. I spread the liquid to my dick while jerking it off. As soon as she was done with orgasm, I continued coming inside. We continued with the action for 20 additional minutes. After that, she was lying on my chest as I kissed her hair.

Chapter 4

After an hour of flying, I could finally see the lights of my city. I was happy to be back there. After what I've been through, I was supposed to take a rest, but I didn't want to rest because I had to work.

I worked for days. I did every kind of experimentation using the plants from the island. Experimentations were for purposes of making a perfect woman perfume that will be turning on men just like that.

I was even more motivated for this project than I was before I crashed with my plane. What made me so motivated was the situation where the plane crashed just after I screwed Lucy.

While I was fucking her, I was feeling the biggest joy that a human being can feel. Just after few minutes when the plane crashed, I was in the worst struggle that a human being can experience.

Being transmitted from the best to the worst, I realized the importance of sex. That was a reason more for me to make this perfume, to make people connect and enjoy their bodies.

I was working really hard and I came up with the first version of it. I was happy, but there was something wrong with my body. During experimentations, I didn't have any sexual activities. I didn't even jerk off. Finally, I decided to jerk it off. After sperm left my genitals, I saw blood on my skin. My dick was bleeding.

I thought it was going to stop, but it didn't. Since it was bleeding plentifully, I had to search for a help. I had one man version of the perfume. I headed to a hospital. I knew that I was going to meet a female nurse, so I sprayed a little bit of my perfume on my neck.

I went to the hospital and as I waited in the raw there were many people there. There was a woman right behind me, and she was really close to my neck.

I could see that she likes it, but I didn't know if it made her turned on. Nevertheless, I entered the room and a female nurse was there.

"I feel a little bit uncomfortable."

"You shouldn't be uncomfortable. Whatever your problem is, we can solve it."

She was sitting next to me when she started looking at my face. She was going to my neck; she was smelling it and she sighed.

"Why are you examining my face even though I didn't tell you where my problem is?"

"I'm sorry, did you say something?" She asked me.

"What's going on nurse?"

"Fuck me."

"What?" Being shocked by what she just said, I asked her this.

"I can't resist this perfume. Oh my god, it's turning me on so much." She sighed as she was saying this.

"I'm not sure if I can have sex now because I'm bleeding down there."

"So that's the problem. We will fix it later, now just go on and fuck me."

"I can't fuck you. It's too bloody down there, I would destroy it."

"Whatever you destroy I will repair later, just screw me."

The emotions of lust and happiness were mixed in me. I was turned on, and at the same time happy because my perfume worked.

She stripped my pants off, and even though it was bleeding, she put him in her mouth and started sucking it. After a few moments, she put him out and spit the blood.

"You see, the blood is gone. Now screw me."

I wanted to look formal, so I decided to wear a suit.

She stripped my suit off. A shirt with a tie were the only things that left. She was pulling my tie as she was sucking it. When she would pull my tie I would come just in front of her head so she would kiss my mouth.

She was doing it alternately. A blood from my penis started to come out. Since she was sucking my dick and then kissing my mouth, the blood would stay on my lips.

She was wearing a skirt and a very tight bodice. The twine that connected two parts of her bodice stretching over the boobs was ripped. I ripped it with my mouth because she turned me on for real. I bit her boobs, and after that, I grabbed my dick and ejaculated on her boobs as blood dripped down her neck and came down to her boobs. After a few minutes of pause, I put it inside her vagina.

"Oh, it's so big. Oh, don't mind. Do not mind my words! Just go as hard as possible. You're a fucking wizard, I've never had bigger and thicker dick inside." Said she.

And I did, I was going as hard as possible as my blood was being left inside her vagina. At the beginning, it was a little bit awkward for me imagining the blood from my penis coming inside her pussy, but now, it's turning me on.

I was so turned on, that I really fucked her. I turned her upside down and laid her on the table. I climbed on the table and started screwing her. It was so good to screw her like that.

I literally destroyed her pussy. She was bleeding too. Our blood mixed up inside her pussy. Finally, I ejaculated on her legs. She was licking the sperm and I was wiping my dick off using her forehead. It was amazing experience. After that, she wrapped my dick in a bandage and took a nice care of it.

Chapter 5

I went back to my house and I continued with my perfume development. I wanted to make few versions of my perfume before starting the sale.

After I made few versions of the perfume, I came up with a nice idea. I was thinking of the women that their husbands cheat on. I wanted to see if this perfume put on their neck will awake a sexual desire toward their respective women. I arranged a meeting with a very popular life coach from my city.

I asked if there are many female clients that come to him because they have problems regarding the loyalty of their husbands. He said that many women get cheated on by their husbands.

I suggested him to recommend my perfume to every woman that gets cheated on by her husband. In return, I offered him some money.

He was thinking that my idea was good, and he agreed. After some time, once again I arranged a meeting with Andrew, the life coach.

"Man, this perfume is amazing. 8 out of 10 women said that this perfume works. Their husbands can't get out of their pussies. The only thing they do is that they go to a job, come home, and they fuck their wives all night long."

I was so proud of what I did. I was planning to start with sale of the perfume. I was thinking about what should my advertising message be like. I realized that it would be the best to relate it to the women that get cheated on by their husbands. Anyway, I couldn't come up with an original advertising message.

After a lot of thinking, I came up with an idea. I started the sale, and it was going very well. I was really proud of myself. Women were buying it like it was the only thing that can arouse sexual desire. The sexual life of many women got better.

They were sending me letters. Andrew's female patients were even coming to my house to thank me. The money I earned, I spent in the clubs, with women, buying clothes and so on.

I was a very confident man trying to be as successful as possible. That's why I didn't stop with this perfume. I was thinking about something else. Something that would improve sex experience.

Chapter 6

While I was watching a documentary about emotions, I've seen a man talking about the problem of expressing emotions. He said that there is not enough of words to express our emotions.

"Vocabularies of the languages are too poor to express every emotion we feel." Said the man.

I came up with an interesting idea. I wanted to make a sexual language that wouldn't use any of the existing words from any of the existent languages. I wanted to explore human psychology and see what are the words or sentences that would come up to people's mind during sexual experience. I wanted to make a language that will only cover the emotions that we feel during sex.

That language will be used to express the emotions deeply and very specifically. Also, it will help people get turned on during sex.

"Fight for freedom of the deepest and most beautiful emotions." I was planning to have this sentence as an advertising message.

However, it wasn't a time to think about advertising message, because I didn't even start making the language.

I realized that it will take a lot of research and lot of struggle to succeed in making such language. This time, once again I met my good friend Andrew. I suggested him to assign a task to his female patients. They should try to think of what they want to say during sex and after they say it, they should remember what, and in which part of their bodies they felt it. Women were coming up with really interesting words.

Every week Andrew would come up with new words to me. I made a pretty interesting list of words. After that, I told Andrew that he should give those words to different women, to the ones that were not included in this project yet.

Those women should use those words in order to see if they can arouse the emotion, and he did what I said. 70 % of the words were successful. Those words managed to awake certain emotions. Days were coming by, business was growing and my confidence grew up.

I decided that I want to organize an orgy. I wanted to assign a task to every participant in the orgy to write down what they feel like saying when they reach certain emotion, that they wouldn't be able to describe by existent words of their respective languages.

There were 10 of us in a large room. I was having sex with tall redhead. She was simply beautiful.

I had some amazing feelings and I described them with some amazing words. When I was fucking her, every time when I was feeling like ejaculating inside, I put him outside to calm the fire down a little bit.

While doing that, I felt a certain emotion, and I found a certain word for it. Every time I would go with my dick between her boobs she would feel something. Sex was all about feelings. After we were done with it, I gathered all of the words and it was time for something big to do. I decided I should make a vocabulary and start selling it.

I gathered all the words that worked and put them into the vocabulary. I made an advertisement message: "Fight for freedom of the deepest and most beautiful emotions."

In a few days, I was ready to release it.

One day, I received a call. Andrew said that there was a woman that has a business idea regarding my project. I headed to Andrew's office and some extremely sexy woman was there. She had a tattooed leg and one couldn't really resist not to disrespect her in a way of looking at her legs, instead of looking at her eyes during a conversation.

Anyway, It was for my business and I had to calm down my emotions. In the middle of the conversation when I really felt like I want to look at her leg and just lick it for a half of an hour, I said:

"Stop, I want to write something down."

I took a paper and a pen, and I wrote a really long word. I said it and I felt like I just described the sexy appeal of her leg. In the middle of the conversation, all of the sudden I was once again in the plane that I was in, when I went to search for the plants.

I was transferred in the moment where I screwed Lucy and two female pilots. Lucy asked me If I want to fuck her once again. I wasn't aware of the fact that last time when I was in that situation we died. Although I wasn't aware of it, I refused to screw her once again

"Hey, you sexy boy. Can you screw me once again?" Asked Lucy.

"No, one time was enough." I answered.

"You didn't like the food that I brought to you, just before you screwed me the first time?"

"No, the food was great. I wasn't hungry."

"Then you don't like me?"

"No, I like you it's just that I had enough."

"All of the sudden, a man knocked on the door of the cockpit."

"Where is the stewardess? I wanted to take my drink but stewardess didn't show up already for an hour and thirty minutes."

I whispered to Lucy: "Hey, Lucy. There is someone that could have sex with you."

She bit her lip and said: "Hey, I'm inside this cockpit and I'm hurt. That is the reason why I can't get to passengers to serve them."

"Can you come in and help me with my injury?"

"I'm coming." Said the man.

When he entered the room and saw that the girls were only wearing clothes for upper part of the body, he didn't know what happens.

"What's going on here, girls?"

"I have an injury down there, and it hurts so much. I had to make my pussy opened to the air to reduce the pain." Said Lucy.

"If you are injured, then why are pilots without their underwear?" Asked the man.

"Because they want to solace me by showing me that I'm not the only one who has to be without pants and underwear." Answered Lucy.

"Can you please come here and take a look at this? Maybe we could together find a solution for my painful situation." Said Lucy.

He came there, she put his hand in her pussy and they started making it out. Not a long time after it, he started to screw her.

I decided to go for a walk

I came to the biggest window of the plane and I took a look down at the ground with my spyglass. I've seen some smoke coming out of some plants. I wondered what was that. The smoke was going straight through the plane and in the room where Lucy and the passenger had an intercourse. The smoke was without a smell. I went to the room where two of them were still having sex, and I have seen that smoke was going straight in their bodies.

Hey, people. Can you see this smoke?

"What smoke? Is everything okay with you?"

"Yes, everything is okay with me. Can't you see the smoke that is going straight inside your bodies?"

"No, I can't." Said the man.

"Eugene, there is no smoke." Said Lucy.

I went back to the window. I've heard the passenger sighing. I realized he was finished. He had an orgasm. The smoke disappeared and I was back in the reality; in the present time.

The woman whom I had the meeting with was sitting in front of me as she asked:

"What did you see?"

I didn't answer her question. I was just looking at the table as I was thinking about what happened. I was thinking about how I got back to the past. I realized that the place where the smoke came from was the island that I was at.

"Tell me immediately, what did you see?"

"I was back in the past."

"I know that you were back in the past. Now tell me, what did you see there?"

"I can't really tell you that."

"Why can't you?"

"Because I am just too shocked to talk about it at this moment."

The woman stood up and headed to the exit door.

"Where are you going?" I asked.

"To the exit door, can't you see?"

"Why are you leaving? What about the business idea?" I asked her.

"It doesn't matter." She said and left the building.

I didn't think much about her. I went back to my house and I started thinking about what happened right there. Why was I brought back in the past and what did all of it mean?.

Chapter 7

I realized that the island is the center of sexual desire. I realized that every time when somebody has sex, it's because the person was turned on.

The person was turned on because the smoke was coming to its body. If there wasn't the smoke and the plants, nobody would have a sexual desire and the world wouldn't be reproducing.

I also realized that my perfume was so successful because I took extracts from those plants and I put it in the perfume.

That way I made the sexual drive from the plants available to people directly, by putting a perfume on the neck.

Since I had a lot of those plants, I decided to plant them on a wide territory to see what's going to happen. In the first few weeks, nothing really happened. After two months, TV channels started talking about natality increment. I realized that by planting so much of those plants, I led the sexual desire in the world to increment. That wasn't everything.

One day, I've seen a square-shaped vehicle in a front of my body. It didn't produce any sound, but it produced some waves that were irritating me so much that I just had to come out of my house.

They were some kind of aliens.

"We heard about you."

"Where did you hear about me? Who are you?"

"We are watching on earth all the time, but we have never been directly influenced by the powers of earth until now.

We are coming from another planet."

I was shocked.

What planet?

"It doesn't really matter. We are here to ask you what is it so special in those plants that they increased natality on our planet?"

I couldn't believe what they just told me. I was a sexual genius. Not only that I was selling the perfumes that were arousing sexual desire in people, but I also increased natality of earth and of other planets. I was also about to sell my vocabulary with sexual language.

"Those plants are the center of sexual desire. Every time when one gets turned on, it gets turned on because the plants allowed him. If those plants didn't exist, neither the life on earth nor the life on the other planets would exist." I explained to the aliens.

"We just wanted to come here to thank you for everything that you did. We had a problem with natality on our planet.

People had a really low sexual drive. Now, everyone wants to have sex. It's just beautiful. During sex, we feel more joy than we felt before. If there is anything we can help you with, or if you need anything just contact us. We will leave you this wave device".

"This way we can communicate with our thoughts which are later transmitted into waves and at the end, into voices. However, I'm not going to have time to tell you about the way this device works, so I will just leave it to you right here."

"There is something that you can help me with. There is a problem on earth. It's getting overcrowded." I said.

"Yes, I get it. People are having much sex and now earth is starting to lack space." Said one of the aliens.

"Exactly, and I wanted to ask you about your planet, can the people from earth somehow start emigrating to your planet? Is it a big planet?"

All four aliens that were there at the moment started laughing.

"Is it big? Did you hear that?" Said the alien that talked to other alien.

"It has infinite space." One of the aliens answered.

"Then, can you make it possible for the people from earth to emigrate there?"

"Why not? You did as a big favor, and we lose nothing by letting the people from earth emigrate to our planet."

After few months, the process of emigrating started.

Whenever earth would get overcrowded, the people from earth would emigrate. Everything was going well. I released my vocabulary about sexual emotions. I was surprised how many people started buying it. I became very popular.

Chapter 8

Everything was going well, until the sexy woman with a business plan didn't show up. I have to confess, I was a little bit scared when I saw her in front of my house.

"Hey, sweetie." She kissed my cheek after she said it.

"Why did you come? Maybe you have a business idea that you don't want to tell me? And if you don't want to tell me, then there is no reason for you to come here." I said with expressions of anger on my face.

"Sweetie, don't be upset. I know that it was impolite to leave just like that, but I realized that I had something really important to do. I came here to make it up to you."

She said while she raised her skirt a little bit. After she did, the whole tattoo was visible on her leg. I was on fire. There is nothing that turns me on like the tattoo. We entered my house. She started kissing me. She stripped me off completely. My sexy beard along with my hair was the only thing that covered my body.

She was just beautiful. I couldn't separate my lips from that tattoo. I was just kissing and licking the tattoo. There were some roses painted on her leg, and it was so hot. I stripped her off completely. I put her hand on my chest. I put it just in the line that separated left and the right side of my chest. I put my tongue between her legs as I was lying in the upside-down position. At the same time, I was licking her vagina and she was sucking my penis. After that, I told her to stand against the wall. I put it inside completely.

"Oh, what's that so big? Tell me, what is that so big?" She asked.

"It's my dick, it's going to destroy your pussy." I answered.

"Ah. Just go on, destroy my pussy. I want to ejaculate. I want you to suck my sperm and then to spit it on the rose that you were kissing previously." She said.

As soon as she said this, I was completely on fire. I fucked her so hard that she started crying.

"Are you sure that you want me to continue? I can see that you shed few tears?" I asked.

"Please, don't stop! Go even harder on me." Said she.

I grabbed her hair and I started going even harder on her.

She ejaculated. Her legs were shaking. Her orgasm lasted for about thirty-five seconds. I suck the liquid from her vagina in my mouth and I spit it on the rose. After that, I ejaculated on her tattoo.

It was just incredible experience.

At the end of sex, I asked her:

"What is the business idea you wanted to suggest me?"

"I wanted to ask you if you can screw me every day like this?"

"Of Course I can." I said while kissed her mouth with my tongue inside it.

I like to write great romance stories that take you on an emotional journey whether tears, laughter (or both) or just steamy hot fun (or all of them).

Please... leave a review, let me know if you had enjoyed read this great story?

THANK YOU ☺

www.ingramcontent.com/pod-product-compliance
Lightning Source LLC
Chambersburg PA
CBHW050911120626
46552CB00004B/1525